TULLY'S BIRTHDAY

Available in the Tales of Tully series

Tully's Life
This heart-warming story follows the journey of Tully from street dog to much-loved family pet, teaching young readers about the importance of kindness, understanding and hope.

Tully Takes Off!
Tully has arrived in her new home with her new grown-up, but she does not like it one bit! When Tully sees an opportunity to go back to her old life on the streets - the only life she has known up to now - she takes it with both paws. With a search underway, it is up to her new grown-up to work out what Tully needs and help get her safely home.

Tully and the Sad Day
Tully has woken up feeling grey and cloudy inside and she does not know what to do. She cannot help her big feeling because she does not know what it is. As her different feelings begin to work together in the wrong way, it is up to Tully's grown-up to help her to understand what she needs.

Go To Sleep Tully!
It is night time and Tully is tired, but she does not want to go to sleep. Her new grown-up knows that Tully is trying every trick she can to avoid going go to bed! With lots of adventures planned and Tully needing her rest, Tully's grown-up needs to find a way to help Tully learn to not be so worried about bedtime.

Tully and the Midnight Feast
Tully is a newly-adopted dog settling in with her new grown-up. Since her arrival, her snacks have started mysteriously disappearing from the cupboard and appearing under her bed, she seems to have forgotten her manners, and there are days when she just cannot stop eating! Tully and her grown-up need to work together to help Tully with her worries about food.

Tully and the Scary Day
Tully has woken up feeling scared. She isn't really sure why, but today feels like a very scary day, and she just wants to hide. Tully's grown-up is thankfully there to help Tully manage her big feelings and see that the day is not so scary after all.

Don't Touch Tully!
Tully is settling in with her new grown-up. She has learned that the new grown-up is a safe person and she enjoys strokes and cuddles with them. Then Tully starts to meet new people, who want to show her how loved she is. Unfortunately, Tully doesn't feel the same about people she does not know and trust. It is up to Tully's grown-up to find a way to help Tully with her big feelings and to be Tully's voice, when she can't use hers.

Tully and the Tummy Ache
Tully has a tummy ache and it's making her feel quite grumpy. She doesn't want to eat or drink, and she can't get comfortable. Her tummy is sore and it's getting worse! Tully is in a toilet muddle. So, Tully and her grown-up work together to sort the muddle out and help Tully to cure her tummy ache.

Tully's Birthday

It's Tully's birthday, and her grown-up has planned a special day for her, but Tully doesn't feel like celebrating. As the day begins to unfold, so do Tully's big feelings. Tully doesn't know what to do about the big feelings, so she does a bad thing. Luckily, Tully's grown-up is there to help her feel better about herself, and enjoy the rest of her birthday.

Listen, Tully!

Tully does not always like to listen, especially when her grown-up is trying to stop her having fun. Tully decides that instead of listening, she can be in charge. But when things start to go wrong, Tully and her grown-up need to work out how Tully can begin to find listening a little bit easier.

Tully and the Makeover

Tully has been having lots of fun playing in the mud, but now her grown-up says she has to have a bath. Oh dear! Tully is not sure she wants one of those. She is feeling a bit nervous about what is going to happen to her, but Tully's grown-up shows her that there is nothing to worry about. Having a bath is a good thing after all.

Tully and Vera

Tully has moved in with her new grown-up but she is missing her foster carer, Vera. Tully is struggling to understand why she had to leave, and whether it is okay to have big feelings about Vera. It is up to Tully's grown-up to try and help her to understand loss and endings and why, sometimes, they have to happen to make space for new beginnings.

Tully and the Chase

Tully loves to be chased. It gives her a feeling of excitement which starts off as being fun, but one day the excited feeling suddenly and very quickly becomes a feeling which is too big. Instead of feeling excited, Tully starts to feel scared. Tully and her grown-up need to work out how they can play Tully's exciting game without it becoming a bit too much for her, and causing a muddle.

Tully at Christmas

Things are starting to feel a bit different in Tully's house and all around outside. Tully's grown-up looks different, strange lights are appearing everywhere and people have started putting their gardens indoors! Tully is not sure what to make of this thing called Christmas – she just wants everything to stay the same. What can Tully's grown-up do to make Christmas-time a nicer time for both of them?

Tully Goes on Holiday

Tully has gone on a holiday with her grown-up. After a difficult start, things seem to be going well. But when the fairground opens up, with all its flashing lights, loud music and food smells, Tully's big feelings get the better of her, making her want to run. And she does! Tully's grown-up needs to find her in time to show her that holidays can be fun after all.

Tully and the New Rules

Tully likes lots of things about living in a house with her grown-up, but one thing she really doesn't like is all the rules! Tully thinks the rules are all very boring and her grown-up must want to stop her from having fun. One day Tully breaks her least favourite rule, and something bad happens. Tully doesn't know what to do! Can Tully's grown-up get to the bottom of this muddle so it doesn't happen again?

Tully's Birthday

TALES OF TULLY

Jess van der Hoech

Trauma Tools & Training

ISBN-13 978-1-06-86917-3-7
Editing by Sarah Ogden
www.jvtraumatools.co.uk

Acknowledgements

As always, to my trusted editor Sarah Ogden for all that you do to make these books come to life. I will never fully know what goes on behind the scenes, but it is a joy to work alongside you on these projects. Thank you.

Thank you to my supervisor Linda Hoggan for your continued support, encouragement, discussion and much-welcomed feedback on this series. I learn so much from you and the knowledge I have gained form our conversations has been invaluable across my practice, the books and now this series. Thank you.

Thank you to Laura Benham, for your support in giving me feedback, the searching questions, your friendship and of course, the countless conversations about dogs, the content of which has become quite useful! Thank you.

To the children and families who I meet in my therapy room, from whom I have learned more about hope and healing than any course could ever teach me. Your input, ideas, questions and answers are so valuable to me and I will be forever grateful. Thank you.

Preface

The *Tales of Tully* series is based on the adoption of an ex street dog from Bosnia who came to live with me in September 2023. Watching her try to settle and adapt from everything she had previously known to fit in with a new way of life began to present a number of ideas as to how to communicate such difficulties that can be experienced, to others who are in the process of adopting or who have adopted children. The aim of the series is to provide an opportunity to explore different situations, circumstances, feelings and experiences, finding new ways of communicating and understanding each other, through the voice of Tully.

For many children who have experienced early trauma, self-esteem, self-belief and self-confidence may not be present. Asking them to speak positively about themselves is like asking them to speak another language. Some children find overt praise quite difficult to handle, and it is more meaningful for them to overhear positive conversations from their grown-ups about them, rather than a big announcement of how wonderful they are.

Sometimes the child may believe one or two good things about themselves; an 'I am' or 'I can' phrase, for example. Often, when I ask a child at the early stages of therapy to tell me the good words about themselves, they suggest something that they perceive as negative – 'I am annoying' for example. They often can't think of a good word to describe themselves.

One thing that the grown-ups can struggle with is that when children are made the centre of attention in what the adult believes is a positive way, they quickly sabotage it. 'Spoiling' their own big birthday party, breaking gifts or becoming reactive when receiving presents or positive attention. When a child feels inherently bad about themselves, celebrating 'them' can feel too much. They believe that they are not worthy or that they don't deserve the good things.

Very sadly, for some children, gifts or praise could be a trigger directly linked to past traumas that have happened, so there are a number of things to take into consideration to understand why praise and feeling good can be a difficult place for a child to get to.

When Tully first came to me, I made sure she had the best and healthiest (and quite expensive) food. She refused it, much to my dismay. I bought her some cheap tins and she loved it; it was what she knew. It was no good for her, but why choose a salad when fish and chips is on offer?! She had a lovely soft and comfortable bed, but she chose the floor in the early days. I gave her a nice blanket which she chewed big holes in, and I won't tell you what she did to the eyes of 'Bear' – a toy passed down from my previous dog. Poor Bear, who had been so lovingly cared for and looked after until then.

I needed to realise that Tully was not aware that she was being a saboteur of all the good things she now had on offer. It was not personal to me that she did not want the food or the bed. She did not know that the blanket was not for chewing and she certainly did not have the sentimental feelings towards Bear that I did!

It was up to me to help Tully to learn. I had to teach her that the blanket is not for chewing, but she can have a chewy bone for that. When I praise her, sometimes she does get a bit over excited still and I end up with a paw in my face. It is up to me to help her to take praise and stay calm, and I need to give her that praise in a measured, quiet way so that she mirrors me.

Building self-esteem can take a lot of time. Small doses of genuine praise are often received much better than the big displays. Some children do respond well to those big displays, and the key is in recognising what the child needs and being prepared to know and accept that important celebrations relating to the child may be tricky at first, but with time, love and patience, self-worth, belief and confidence can all improve.

How to use this book

First and foremost, ensure that both you and the child are well-regulated and comfortable when you begin to read Tully's story. Make sure you choose a time when you are unlikely to be interrupted. The child may like a soother, a favourite or fidget toy, a drink or something to suck or chew to help them to stay regulated.

If the child is calm, then begins to try and distract or move away from the reading, make a note of what they have just heard in the text. It is very likely that they will have just provided you with some valuable information about something that they cannot tolerate or want to avoid for now.

The questions have been designed not only to explore the internal world of the child, but to help to develop a common language between the child and adult who are using this book together. The child cannot get the answers to the questions incorrect. Their interpretation of the thoughts and feelings Tully is having may provide some very significant information about the child's own thoughts and feelings. The child may want to expand the answers to talk about themselves and may even be able to make comparisons between Tully's feelings and their own.

Tully's Birthday

It was a lovely day. The sun was shining, the birds were singing and Tully's grown-up was very excited. It was a special day for Tully. It was her birthday.

Is Tully excited about her birthday?

Why is Tully's grown-up excited for her birthday?

Tully had woken up to find some gifts waiting for her. Her grown-up sat with her and opened them. She had a new chewy bone, a sparkly collar and a new puzzle toy that she could get treats from. The gifts gave Tully big feelings.

What feelings might Tully have about getting lots of gifts?

Tully's grown-up had invited Tully's friend Stella round for a special birthday tea. When Stella and her grown-up arrived, they were all going to go on a walk together and then come home for some delicious dinner.

It all felt a bit too much for Tully.

Why might Tully be finding the day a bit hard?

Tully's grown-up was happy and excited for Tully's birthday and had organised all of these special things for her.

But nobody had celebrated Tully's birthday like this before and it felt confusing for Tully. Tully's last birthday had been spent at a shelter in Bosnia with her foster family. Before that, Tully had been a street dog and lived on her own.

Remembering her last birthday gave Tully big feelings in her body and she decided at that moment to go and chew a hole in the sofa.

Why might Tully have decided to chew the sofa?

How does Tully feel about her birthday?

Tully chewed and chewed and the hole got bigger and bigger. Suddenly, Tully realised what she had done.

Tully's big feelings were even bigger now because she knew she had done a bad thing.

When Tully had lived in Bosnia as a street dog, she did not have a special person of her own to take care of her. Some people had given Tully and her body big hurts. This had made Tully believe that she was a bad girl.

What big feelings might Tully have?

Is Tully a bad girl?

Tully did not think she deserved all of the nice things her grown-up did for her. Sometimes, she did something that she knew was wrong because she wanted her grown-up to be cross with her. Now, she thought her grown-up was cross with her.

"Oh Tully!" her grown-up said sounding very disappointed.

Tully was worried that she had done a bad thing and would be sent away again.

What other worries might Tully have?

Tully's grown-up knew that Tully had big feelings and felt like a bad girl. Tully's grown-up also knew that Tully had a good heart and that when she was small, the bad things that had happened to her were very wrong. The bad things were not Tully's fault. Tully's grown-up wanted her to know that she had always had a good heart.

Every day, Tully's grown-up told her all of the good words about herself. Tully is very loyal and loving, fun and playful. Tully is very special and loved. Sadly, Tully did not believe the good words about herself just yet.

What good words would your grown-ups say about you?

Later that day, Stella and her grown-up arrived for the walk and the birthday tea. There was even a special doggy birthday cake! When they had finished their walk and eaten the food, Stella and Tully went to play in the garden.

Later, Tully came back inside and overheard the grown-ups talking.

"I know that Tully has a good heart and she is a good girl. I would like to help her to believe all the good things about herself that I can see in her."

What can Tully's grown-up do to help Tully believe the good words about herself?

Tully thought about what she had done that morning and wanted to make it right. After Stella and her grown-up had gone home, Tully dragged her blanket to the sofa and used it to cover up the hole she had chewed.

Why might Tully have done this?

"Oh Tully!" her grown-up said. "I can see you want to make this right. I know you have big feelings and I am here to help you. If you let me know you have a big feeling and need some help, I will help you. Instead of chewing the sofa, if you need to chew, you can chew this." Tully's grown-up gave her the new chewy bone.

"If you need to run, I can take you to the field so you can run. If you need me to sit with you, I can do that too.

"Sometimes, you do something that I am not pleased with, but I still love you. I always love you, even if I look cross and grumpy, I still love you. Other feelings come and go, but love will always stay.

"And you will always stay too Tully, you're not going anywhere! I will always keep you safe."

Tully knew now why her grown-up wanted to celebrate her birthday with her.

Because Tully is loved.

About the author

Jess van der Hoech is a qualified therapist who has spent the last ten years studying and working with the impact of developmental trauma and, in particular, the assessment and treatment of children and adolescents with complex trauma and dissociation.

As well as supporting birth families, Jess works with looked-after and adopted children and families, using skills in attachment-focused therapy and therapeutic parenting techniques.

Jess is a supervisor, trainer and motivational speaker with a passion for writing therapeutic books that are accessible to children and families to help with the healing process and to increase awareness in the impact of trauma.

Jess van der Hoech

Also by Jess van der Hoech

What A Muddle (2016) ISBN 978 18381987 0 1 (Co-authored with Renée Potgieter Marks)
An interactive, practical workbook designed to help children who have difficulties with emotional regulation to begin to understand what is happening in their bodies. A variety of activities throughout the book enable the child to start to explore these ideas through the story of Sam, while gently encouraging them to begin to verbalise their own experiences. Carrying out the physical exercises in the book can promote changes in emotional regulation. The text is written in a child-friendly, gender-neutral style, and is easy to understand for parents, carers and practitioners alike. For children aged 4-12.

These Three Words (2018) ISBN 978 18381987 5 6
Also available as an e-book. A unique therapeutic novel for teenagers with the aim of linking together the feelings, emotions and behaviours connected to anxiety, with some of the therapeutic tools that can be used in order to enable better self-regulation, increased confidence and different ways of thinking. The book is equally valuable to parents of teenagers with anxiety, giving them an insight and understanding into some of the issues that may be affecting their child, and potentially opening up a line of communication and a way forward between parent and teen.

These Three Words: The Journal (2019) ISBN 978 18381987 2 5
A thought-provoking and hands-on workbook, combining a series of practical exercises and tools designed to assist teenagers who are struggling with the symptoms of anxiety. Addressing the anxious responses in both brain and body, this journal provides the reader with the opportunity to discover therapeutic coping techniques and learn how to apply them to their own personal problem areas, before committing to a twenty-eight-day practice to promote good emotional regulation and reduced anxiety. The journal can be used alongside the therapeutic novel These Three Words, or as a standalone workbook, and it is suitable for use by the teenage reader on their own, with a parent, or in a group.

Beastie, Baby and the Brand-New Mummy (2022) ISBN 978 18381987 3 2 and *Beastie, Baby and the Brand-New Daddy (2022) ISBN 978 18381987 4 9*
A therapeutic story that looks at the external signs of pathological dissociation in a child. Dolly's story helps children who have experienced early trauma to begin to understand, in a very simple way, what dissociation is and why it has happened in their internal world. Tools and techniques are included within the story that parents and caregivers can use to assist the child in the first stages of their healing process. Beautiful illustrations on every page enhance the story of Dolly, and help the reader to relate to the events that happen, to notice the methods Dolly has developed to manage her feelings, and to think about what is happening in their own internal world. For children aged 4-12

Printed in Great Britain
by Amazon

62815711R00020